THE TOTALLY NINJA RACCOONS MEET BIGFOOT

by Kevin Coolidge

Illustrated by Jubal Lee

The Totally Ninja Raccoons Are:

Rascal:
He's the shortest brother and loves doughnuts. He's great with his paws and makes really cool gadgets. He's a little goofy and loves both his brothers, even when they pick on him, but maybe not right then.

Bandit:
He's the oldest brother. He's tall and lean. He's super smart and loves to read. He leads the Totally Ninja Raccoons, but he couldn't do it by himself.

Kevin:
He may be the middle brother, but he refuses to be stuck in the middle. He has the moves and the street smarts that the Totally Ninja Raccoons are going to need, even if it does sometimes get them into trouble as well as out of trouble.

CONTENTS

"Someone ate all the pork out of the pork-fried rice."

1

TOTALLY NINJA

A furry head pops up from a trash can, the lid tilted on his head like a hat. It's a raccoon, and he's holding a box of Chinese takeout. "Someone ate all the pork out of this pork-fried rice, and there aren't any chopsticks!" says Kevin.

The trashcan beside the raccoon starts to tremble noisily. There's no lid, so when a voice from within calls out, it echoes. "Who would throw away doughnuts? I love doughnuts," says the voice.

Another raccoon pokes his head up over the rim. It's Rascal. There is a jelly doughnut in his mouth, the powder speckling his face and whiskers. His whiskers twitch.

"Here are your chopsticks, bro," a voice from the third trashcan calls out. End over end, a pair of chopsticks flies across the cans as many other objects come flying out: a banana peel, an orange rind, a broken toaster.

"Haven't these people heard of junk food?" asks Bandit. Rascal turns his furry face just in time for the chopsticks to hit him in the forehead. The wooden chopsticks bounce off his head. Kevin's little, black paw reaches out to snatch them from the air.

"Oh look! General Tso's chicken!" says Kevin excitedly as he glances back down into the trash can.

"Hey, if the general threw it away, he must not want it anymore," answers Rascal.

"No, General Tso's chicken is a sweet, slightly spicy, deep-fried chicken dish," says Bandit as he peers over at Kevin's chicken.

"What is he the general of?" asks Rascal.

"Huh? Why, nothing. It's all marketing," replies Bandit.

Rascal dives down for another delicious jelly doughnut. Bandit rests his chin on his paws. His ears twitch.

A screen door slams. Bandit quietly slips back down into the trash can. A bright beam of light shines through the night and stops on Kevin just as he's cramming a huge piece of chicken into his mouth. Kevin grins sheepishly and offers the piece of chicken.

"Get out of my garbage, you stinking thieves," yells a fat, hairy man holding a broom.

With a crash, Bandit's trash can topples over, and he dashes out, running for the safety of the dark. Kevin raises his arms, sniffs and looks puzzled, "I don't smell anything except General Tso's chicken." He jumps out of his trash can and follows Bandit.

"Hey guys, I can't get out. I'm stuck!" shouts Rascal in a muffled voice. The trash can shakes and then stops.

The big, angry man cautiously approaches the can. He's holding a flashlight; his chin jiggles as he shakes a broom in his other hand.

"I told you little bandits that if I caught you in my garbage one more time, I was going to clean house," he yells as he tries to peer into the garbage can. His belly is so huge that it blocks his view.

"The General threw away his chicken and his doughnuts. It's fair game, and my name is Rascal, not Bandit," says a muffled voice from the bottom of the trash can.

Kevin and Bandit stop their scurrying towards the woods and look at each other. "We have to help our clumsy brother," says Bandit. Kevin nods as they run back to the trash can.

Bandit dashes towards the upset man--as he nears the man he starts a series of flips. He vaults onto the trash can, knocking it over. He jumps into the air, and over the man's head.

Bandit grabs the broom handle and flips over the man. It's a great view. He can see the shiny, bald spot on the top of the man's head. He lands behind the man and whacks him in his butt with the end of the broom.

Kevin sprints to the trash can and reaches in with his paws to help his brother. Rascal is stuck. He only comes halfway out. "It looks like you've eaten a few too many doughnuts," says Kevin.

Kevin grunts and pulls really hard. Rascal comes out with a loud, popping sound, and both of them go tumbling backward in a somersault resulting in a heap of fur.

The loud, obese man gives a surprised yell, and the raccoons laugh and go scurrying into the forest.

"That was fun!" exclaimed Kevin as he rubs his paws furiously back and forth.

"I didn't think so. I got stuck, and there are still doughnuts left. I'm also not a thief," Rascal complains.

"You are wearing a mask," says Kevin.

"You have a mask!" shouts Rascal.

"We all have masks, but why be common thieves when we can be... ninjas!" exclaims Bandit.

"I could totally be a ninja," says Kevin.

"What's a ninja?" asks Rascal.

"A ninja is highly trained in martial arts and stealth. Ninjas hire themselves out for secret missions," says Bandit.

"Do ninjas eat General Tso's Chicken?" asks Kevin.

"A ninja eats whatever he wants," replies Bandit.

"I could totally be a ninja!" yells Rascal.

"We are the Totally Ninja Raccoons!" shout the raccoon brothers, jumping and slapping their paws together.

"If we are going to be ninjas, we are going to need the tools of the trade."

2

TOOLS OF THE TRADE

Sunlight shines through the broken window of a super-secret clubhouse. It reveals a bookcase filled with books, odd pieces of junk, and the three raccoon brothers relaxing.

Kevin is lying in his hammock. Rascal is sitting at a table tinkering with an old toaster, and Bandit is sitting on his bed reading a book.

“If we are going to be ninjas, we are going to need the tools of the trade,” says Bandit as he turns a page.

“I already have tools,” Rascal says as he holds up the rusty screwdriver he’s using to take apart the toaster.

“No, silly, he means cool, ninja weapons,” says Kevin as he rubs his little, black paws together.

"Yes, like swords, and grappling hooks, and smoke bombs, but it is also important to have the knowledge and skill to use these tools," says Bandit.

"Ha, Kevin has stink bombs after eating all of General Tso's Chicken. Pee-yoo, the General is going to be maaaad," says Rascal holding his nose with one paw and waving the other around.

"He threw the chicken away!" answers Kevin.

"Guys, guys, we need to focus!" says Bandit, as he waves his paws around, trying to get Kevin's and Rascal's attention.

"I already have mine," says Kevin, as he holds up a long piece of wood.

"That's just a broom handle!" says Bandit.

"It is not. It's a staff. I'm going to clean this town up," says Kevin.

"Ha, the bad guys are toast!" jokes Rascal as he points the toaster he's been working on at Kevin.

Two pieces of well-browned toast pop out and fly across the room. Kevin quickly blocks with the staff and the toast bounces off. Kevin reaches out and grabs one, and takes a bite. Bandit grabs the other.

"Needs raspberry jam," mumbles Kevin through a mouthful of toast. Little crumbs cover his chin.

"And butter," says Bandit. Bandit wipes crumbs off his furry belly.

"What are you going to use for a weapon, Bandit?" asks Rascal.

"I'm the brains of this outfit. I'll use books and observation... and this cool sword I found in the junkyard," says Bandit.

Bandit pulls a long, shiny sword from underneath his bed and holds it up. The point just barely pokes Kevin's hammock and his butt.

"Ouch! Watch where you're pointing that thing!" yells Kevin.

"We have masks. We have weapons. We're totally ready to be ninjas!" yell Kevin, Rascal, and Bandit.

"We can read the want ads in the Wellsboro Gazette."

3

FINDING A JOB

Rascal is rummaging through a trash heap looking for parts. He tosses an old tin can over his shoulder, which Kevin hits like a baseball.

The can soars through the air, spinning end over end, and heads towards the junkyard fence.

“Going, going, and it’s out of here!” shouts Kevin as he throws his paws up in excitement, accidentally hitting Bandit in the back of the head.

“Owww! Watch where you are swinging that staff!” shouts Bandit as he rubs the back of his head. “We still have a lot of hard work to become skilled ninjas,” he says.

“Sorry, bro, I’ll be more careful. Still, if this ninja thing doesn’t work out, I could always play baseball for the Phillies,” says Kevin.

"So, now that we are ninjas, what do we do?" asks Rascal.

"Cool ninja stuff, like fighting bad guys and eating Chinese takeout food," says Kevin as he thrusts out with his staff.

"First, we have to find a job and someone willing to pay us," says Bandit.

"How do we do that?" asks Rascal.

"I know! Let's go knock on some doors!" says Kevin.

"Hold on there. We can read the want ads in the Wellsboro Gazette, and on the Internet. No one knows you are a raccoon ninja on the Internet," says Bandit.

"I want to be a ninja, not a librarian," says Kevin.

Rascal picks up a wrinkled newspaper from a pile of trash. The paper rustles as he opens it. "Oh, here's a double coupon for a box of doughnuts," says Rascal.

"Oh, look. There's a new Chinese restaurant open. We should check out the alley in back tonight," says Kevin as he scratches his back with the staff.

"Give me that paper," says Bandit as he snatches the paper from Rascal. "This is what I'm talking about," says Bandit as he opens the paper to the help wanted ads. He starts reading aloud to Kevin and Rascal.

> *Super genius seeks minions to be quiet and follow orders, do the heavy lifting, work long hours, and change my litter pan. Seeing me happy and ruling Earth is its own reward. Light refreshments will be provided. No dental. Dogs and ferrets need not apply. Call 1-800-takeover.*

"What's a minion?" asks Rascal scratching his head.

"It's a follower of a powerful person," replies Bandit.

"I was thinking of something easier. I have a lot of inventing to do," says Rascal.

"Well, we aren't experienced ninjas... at least not yet, and there are snacks," says Kevin.

"Snacks?! Count me in!" yells Rascal.

"Let's call the number, because we are..." Bandit starts.

"The Totally Ninja Raccoons!" yell Bandit, Kevin, and Rascal.

"When I rule the world, the mailman will deliver me a snack every day."

4

GYPSY PLOTS

A fat, calico cat stares out the window of a large, white house. She's trying to sleep, but the little girl across the street keeps bouncing a ball in the driveway.

"When I'm in charge, there will be no playing with silly toys and keeping me awake. That noisy child will scratch my ears, and my butt. She must remain quiet," meows the fat cat.

She closes one eye, but keeps one open to watch the approaching mailman. Thump, thump, thump, the man walks loudly across the wooden porch.

Every day he comes, except on Sunday. There's no post on Sundays. I loathe Sundays, and my butt itches, thought Gypsy.

"When I run the world, the mailman will deliver

me a snack every day, even on Sunday. Hmmmm, I think Sundays will be sardines, and he'll wear slippers--cute, fluffy, bunny slippers.

"Yes, today, the neighborhood; tomorrow, the world. Right after I take a little nap," meows the fat cat who was called Gypsy by the people who thought they owned the house.

Gypsy puts her head down to start her seventh nap of the day when the phone rings. Gypsy opens one eye and reaches out a paw to pick up the phone.

"Hello, Feline Enterprises, bringing world domination to your doorstep. How can I deceive you?" asks Gypsy as she inspects her claws.

From the phone comes a voice, "I'm calling about the minion position," says Bandit.

"Yes, yes, I'm still looking for slaves. I mean--minions," says Gypsy.

"We're ninjas looking for a job," says Kevin.

"Just how many of you are there?" asks Gypsy.

"Three!" shout Kevin, Bandit, and Rascal into the phone.

"It's all you will need because..." says Bandit.

"We're the Totally Ninja Raccoons!" shout Rascal, Bandit, and Kevin in unison.

"Great, meet me at my secret lair. Here's the address. Don't be late. I will not tolerate tardiness," says Gypsy.

"We're ninja raccoons. We're never tardy!" shouts Bandit.

"What's tardy mean?" whispers Rascal.

"It means running late," says Kevin.

"Oh, I don't like to run. My legs are short," says Rascal.

"Your first mission is to capture Bigfoot."

5

SUPER SECRET MISSION

"Your handwriting is terrible. Are you sure you wrote the address down correctly?" asks Kevin.

"Yes, I wrote it with my invisible pen...in code," says Rascal.

"Why? No one can read it," says Bandit.

"Exactly!" says Rascal.

The ninja raccoons enter an enormous cave. There's a big, wooden desk with a plump cat sitting on top. A large, red button is next to her.

"Welcome, ninja raccoons. Your first mission is to capture the elusive Bigfoot," says Gypsy.

"Bigfoot is just a myth," says Kevin.

"I assure you he's very real, and his tracks have been spotted right here in Wellsboro," says Gypsy.

"Why do you want to capture Bigfoot?" asks Bandit.

"Bigfoot is a menace. Once I control his power of invisibility and stealth, the world will be a much safer place," purrs Gypsy.

"It sounds like you want to be a ninja," says Kevin.

"Yes, exactly like a ninja, only with naps, and snacks, and post even on Sunday," purrs Gypsy.

"But... It's Bigfoot. He's big, and he's scary," says Rascal.

"I'm sorry. I thought I was talking to the Totally Ninja Raccoons? If you aren't up to the job, I can find someone else," says Gypsy.

"We'll take the job," says Bandit quickly.

"Good, good, capture the Bigfoot and bring him back here. Lock him up in that cage over there," says Gypsy, as she points her paw at a cage with big, iron bars, over in the corner.

"We can totally do this because..." shouts Bandit.

"We're the Totally Ninja Raccoons!" shout Kevin, Rascal, and Bandit. Kevin pulls out a smoke bomb, and when the smoke clears, the raccoons are gone.

Gypsy coughs and waves her paws around. "Silly raccoons, once I have Bigfoot in my possession, I can study his power of invisibility and learn all his secrets. Then, I will be on my way to world domination!" says Gypsy.

“The Raccoons hide behind some nearby bushes.”

6

TRACKING BIGFOOT

"According to my research, Bigfoot was last seen right in this area," says Bandit.

"I don't see anything," says Kevin.

"You should get yourself a set of super-duper glasses like mine. I can see for miles and miles," says Rascal as his glasses slide down his nose.

Kevin reaches over and pushes them back into place. The glasses magnify Rascal's eyes, making them look huge and goofy.

"Your eyes are the size of oranges! Hey, that reminds me, did we pack any oranges? I'm hungry!" shouts Kevin.

"Shhhh, we're sneaking," whispers Bandit.

Rascal walks along admiring the birds in the sky. Why, he can actually count the feathers on their wings! He trips and goes sprawling to the ground; his special glasses fly off his furry head.

"Have a nice trip?" laughs Kevin.

"Very funny," grumbles Rascal. Rascal stands up and brushes leaves and twigs off. He bends over to pick up his glasses, and notices something.

"I think Bigfoot was here," says Rascal.

"How do you know?" asks Kevin.

"Because here are his footprints!" yells Rascal. Rascal points to the ground and Kevin and Bandit rush over to see the set of deeply indented prints.

"Those are huge! I could go swimming in those. This Bigfoot guy must be a giant!" says Kevin.

Bandit pulls a book about traps out of his backpack. "Perfect, we'll set up the trap here and wait for night," says Bandit.

Kevin takes rope out of his backpack, and throws part of the rope over a tree branch in a long line. Bandit opens the book and starts to read, and Rascal starts gathering leaves.

"Did you bring the bait?" asks Bandit.

"I did," answers Rascal. Rascal pulls out a banana, a doughnut, and a bottle of birch beer.

"Here, we better put out some General Tso's chicken just to be sure," says Kevin.

The raccoons hide behind some nearby bushes.

"And now we wait," says Bandit.

"I AM Bigfoot," says the little, furry creature.

7

BIG PROBLEMS

"Do you hear that?" asks Bandit.

"Yeah, Kevin is snoring," says Rascal.

There's a loud rustling sound and a surprised yelp. It sounds like the trap is sprung! Someone is shouting for help!

"Help! Somebody help me!" shouts out a deep voice.

"Ha, we caught him! We caught Bigfoot!" yells Kevin.

"I hope he didn't drink the birch beer. I'm thirsty," says Rascal. "Let's collect our prisoner so we can get paid," says Bandit.

"And eat supper. I'm hungry." says Rascal.

The raccoons come running around the bush to see what they have trapped. There, hanging upside-down, is a furry, little creature with huge feet.

"Hey there, raccoons. Help me down from here," says the little creature with the deep voice.

"We're the Totally Ninja Raccoons," says Bandit.

"Well, I'm totally stuck here, so can you give me some help?" asks the creature.

"We're trying to catch the elusive Bigfoot. Have you seen him?" asks Rascal.

"Awwww, this little guy hasn't seen Bigfoot. Let's call it a night and go home," says Kevin.

"I AM Bigfoot!" says the little, furry creature.

"I thought you'd be--uhhhh--taller," says Bandit.

"I'm called Bigfoot, not Tall Foot," says Bigfoot.

"You are our prisoner now. We are taking you to Gypsy, the cat," says Bandit.

"Noooo! Not Gypsy, the cat. She's the head of the super, secret Cat Board and she is planning to take over the world! She's been after me for a long time," says Bigfoot.

"Sorry, but we took the job. We're ninja raccoons for hire," says Bandit.

"You don't understand. You are not cats. There is no place for you in Gypsy's world. Once she has my secrets of invisibility, she'll be well on her way to taking over the world," says Bigfoot.

"You can't be that sneaky. We caught you easy," says Kevin.

"I was thirsty, and I really like birch beer," says Bigfoot.

"Me too!" says Rascal.

"We have to take you in. We don't get paid until we do," says Bandit.

"You'll be next. Gypsy's evil. She won't rest until the entire world is hers. Don't trust her!" yells Bigfoot.

"She's not evil. She has doughnuts," says Rascal.

"And fruit punch," says Kevin.

"Wrap him up, Totally Ninja Raccoons. We've done our part. Now, let's take him in," says Bandit.

"We are the Totally Ninja Raccoons!" yell Kevin, Bandit and Rascal.

"I see you caught the elusive Bigfoot."

8

BIGGER PROBLEMS

"Give me a high five, guys! We'll take Bigfoot back to Gypsy, and get our money!" says Kevin as he puts out his paw.

"I'm going to buy an ice cold birch beer with my portion of the money," says Rascal.

"I have been interested in that book on werewolves," says Bandit.

"There's no such thing as werewolves," says Kevin.

"Mfffph, mfffph," mumbles Bigfoot from the big sack that the raccoons are dragging in through the cave's entrance.

"What's he saying?" asks Kevin.

"He's saying werewolves are real," says Bandit.

“I see you caught the elusive Bigfoot. Hmmm, I always thought he’d be taller,” says Gypsy.

“hmmmpf, wummmpf,” mumbles Bigfoot.

“Would you please take that bag off his head? I can’t understand what he’s saying,” says Gypsy.

“I’m called Bigfoot, not Tall Foot,” says Bigfoot after Kevin takes the bag off his head.

“We did our job, and we’d like to get paid now,” says Bandit.

“And we’d like our snacks,” says Rascal.

“And fruit punch,” says Kevin.

“Do you happen to have any birch beer?” asks Bigfoot.

“I AM Gypsy, the cat. I am head of the Cat Board. I do NOT pay my minions. Now, put that little Bigfoot in the cage and be quiet,” says Gypsy.

“But, there was a promise of snacks!” says Rascal.

“And Chinese food!” shouts Kevin.

“We do a job; we get paid,” says Bandit.

“I told you not to trust her!” says Bigfoot.

Gypsy moves her paw over to the big, red button on her desk. "If you don't hand over the little Bigfoot, I'll hit this big, button and unleash my robot guards, and then you will all be my prisoners," meows Gypsy.

Rascal holds up a large mass of wires from his backpack. "You can push it all you want, but it's not going to do anything without these wires. I kind of borrowed them the last time we were here," says Rascal.

"Nooooooo!" cries Gypsy.

Bandit pulls his sword out and slashes Bigfoot's rope bonds. Kevin pulls a bomb from out of his backpack and throws it.

"Ugggh, what's that smell?" asks Bigfoot.

"Oooops, sorry, wrong pocket. That was the stink bomb," says Kevin.

Kevin throws a smoke bomb. The room fills with smoke, and when the smoke clears, the Totally Ninja Raccoons are gone and Gypsy has tears in her eyes.

"Those darn raccoons! And it stinks in here!"

"I have to go back to the woods."

9

GOODBYE BIGFOOT

"I want to thank you for cutting me loose," says Bigfoot.

"Yeah, you were right. Gypsy is evil, and we don't ninja for free," says Bandit.

"We didn't get any doughnuts or fruit punch," says Rascal.

"Not even any pork-fried rice with the pork already gone," says Kevin.

"I have to go back to the woods. I have to hide from Gypsy. You better watch yourselves. Gypsy will be after you," says Bigfoot.

"We're ninjas. We'll be fine," says Bandit.

"You have a long way to go before you are truly skilled ninjas," says Bigfoot.

"We'll work really hard and become the best raccoon ninjas we can be," says Bandit.

"Besides, Gypsy is lazy, and she doesn't know where we live," says Kevin.

"She's a evil mastermind, and head of the Cat Board," warns Bigfoot.

"We'll just keep our masks on," says Rascal.

"Uhhh, we can't take our masks off," says Kevin.

"It doesn't matter. She'll know it's you. She'll capture you and learn all your secrets," warns Bigfoot.

"No way! We are the Totally Ninja Raccoons!" shout Kevin, Bandit and Rascal...

The End

About the Author

Kevin resides in Wellsboro, just a short hike from the Pennsylvania Grand Canyon. When he's not writing, you can find him at *From My Shelf Books & Gifts*, an independent bookstore he runs with his wife, several helpful employees, and two friendly cats, Huck & Finn.

He's recently become an honorary member of the Cat Board, and when he's not scooping the litter box, or feeding Gypsy her tuna, he's writing more stories about the Totally Ninja Raccoons. Be sure to catch their next big adventure, *The Totally Ninja Raccoons Meet the Weird and Wacky Werewolf.*

You can write him at:

From My Shelf Books & Gifts
7 East Ave., Suite 101
Wellsboro PA 16901

www.wellsborobookstore.com

About the Illustrator

Jubal Lee is a former Wellsboro resident who now resides in sunny Florida, due to his extreme allergic reaction to cold weather.

He is an eclectic artist who, when not drawing raccoons, thunderbirds, and the like, enjoys writing, bicycling, and short walks on the beach.

About Bigfoot

Bigfoot, also known as Sasquatch, is an ape-like creature of American folklore that is said to live in forests or in the mountains. Bigfoot is described as a large, hairy creature that walks on two legs, just like a person. There have been Bigfoot sightings for hundreds of years.

Bigfoot is known by other names too. Sasquatch is the name the Indians gave Bigfoot. The name sasquatch comes from the Native American word sesquac, meaning "wild man". In other countries, like Tibet, he is known as Yeti, or The Abominable Snowman.

Bigfoot doesn't hurt people. He is shy and doesn't like getting close to people. He doesn't like his photo taken. Bigfoot researchers say Bigfoot eats nuts, berries, fish and deer. He's anywhere from six to ten feet tall and can weigh up to 500 pounds.

Most scientists don't believe Bigfoot is real, and consider him to be a combination of folklore, myth, and hoax rather than a real creature. This is because of a lack of physical evidence. Sightings are thought to be other animals, such as black bears.

Do you think Bigfoot is real? Can such a creature exist in today's world? Is there a hairy, wild man alive and running through the woods? Or is it just a story and legend? Investigate, read more, become a reading ninja, and decide for yourself.